CONSTRUCTI
TRUCKS

Grosset & Dunlap

Published by Grosset & Dunlap, a division of Penguin Putnam Books for Young Readers, New York.
GROSSET & DUNLAP is a trademark of Penguin Putnam Inc. Published simultaneously in Canada.
Printed in the U.S.A.

Library of Congress Cataloging-in-Publication Data
Dussling, Jennifer.
    Construction trucks / by Jennifer Dussling ; illustrated by Courtney.
        p.   cm. — (All aboard books)
    Summary: Describes the jobs which various kinds of trucks and other construction equipment do on
a work site.
    1. Trucks—Juvenile literature. 2. Construction equipment—Juvenile literature. [1. Trucks.
2. Construction equipment.] I. Courtney, ill. II. Series: Grosset & Dunlap reading railroad book.
    TL230.15.D87   1998
    629.225—dc21
                                                                                        98-8668
                                                                                        CIP
                                                                                        AC
ISBN 0-448-41885-1   2008 Printing

CONSTRUCTION TRUCKS

By Jennifer Dussling
Illustrated by Courtney

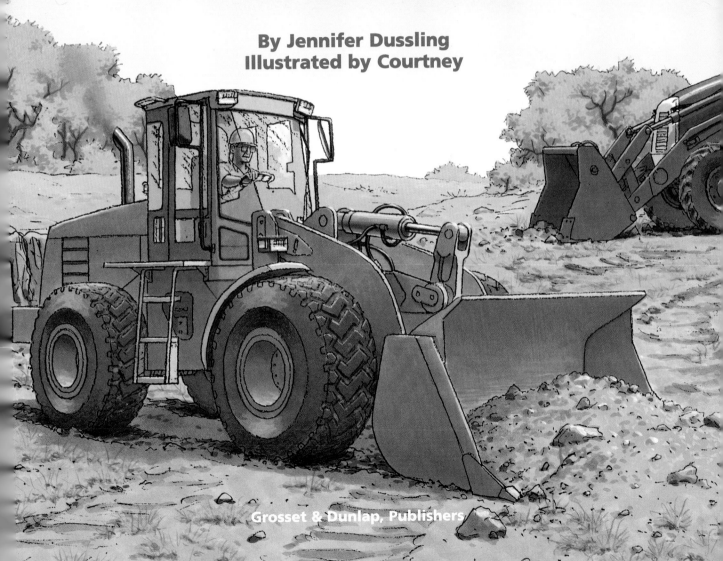

Grosset & Dunlap, Publishers

Welcome to a construction site! Nothing is happening here yet, but someone has bought this land and drawn up plans for a house. Soon it will be filled with construction trucks. A year from now, a house will stand right here, and a family will be living in it.

First, bulldozers clear the site for the new house. A bulldozer's heavy steel blade rips boulders out of the ground. A bulldozer doesn't have wheels like a truck or a car. Instead, it has tracks like a tank. The thick, rubber treads on the tracks help the bulldozer grip rough earth and also can keep it from sinking in soft mud.

Sometimes a bulldozer has a ripper on the back,
like this one. A ripper looks like a giant tooth.
It tears through hard ground.

After the bulldozer clears away rocks and trees, equipment is brought in to dig a hole in the ground. This hole is for the foundation, the support structure of the building. The foundation also will be the house's basement.

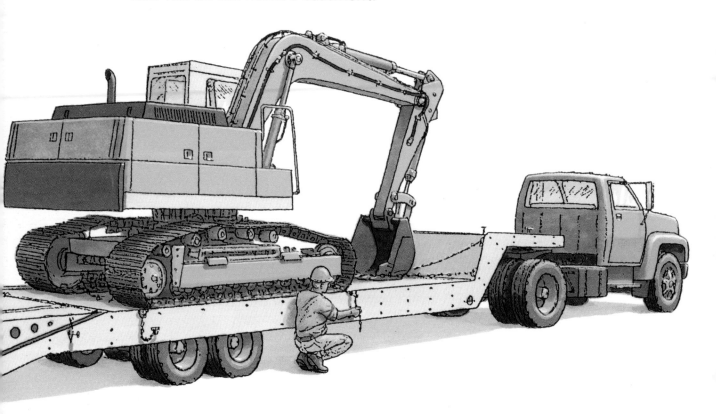

With the bucket at the end of its long metal arm, a backhoe cuts deep trenches in the ground and scoops out loads of dirt. Like a bulldozer, the backhoe has two tracks instead of wheels. The upper part of a backhoe swivels around over the tracks. It can dig on any side, or dig on one side and dump on the other.

A payloader helps the backhoe dig the hole for the foundation. The payloader pushes through dirt, collects it in its wide bucket, raises the load up, and drops it in a dump truck.

A backhoe loader is a cross between a backhoe and a payloader. It has a backhoe on one end and a payloader on the other!

The backhoe and payloader fill the dump truck with dug-up dirt and rock. Dump trucks are very strong. A small dump truck, like this one, carries about a ton of dirt, but a large dump truck can hold more than 100 tons—that's like carrying seventeen elephants!

Rolling on large, rugged tires, the dump truck takes the dirt and rock away from the construction site. When the truck gets to its unloading spot, its back end tilts up so the load can slide off.

When the hole for the foundation is finished, a concrete mixer pours the walls and the floor of the basement. The back of the concrete mixer looks like a barrel on its side that turns around and around without stopping. Why does the back of the truck keep turning? Concrete is a mixture of cement, sand, and gravel that hardens as it dries. By turning around and around, the barrel keeps the concrete from hardening on the way to the building site.

Carpenters take over after the concrete for the foundation is poured. They build the walls, the floors, and the roof with tools like saws and hammers and drills. But the owner of the house has one more idea that needs a very special truck. She wants to move a big tree from her old house to this new one.

The four steel blades of a tree spade burrow under the tree and lift it out, roots and all. The tree is brought to the new house, and the tree spade lowers the tree into a hole it has already dug. The tree will look like it's always been there!

Here is a different kind of construction site. A new road is going to run through this area. Which trucks are used to make a road?

After a bulldozer clears away small trees and bushes, a motor grader comes through. The motor grader has a long blade mounted on its underside. This blade drags over the ground, leveling it and smoothing it out. Soon the ground is flat enough to pave.

Some roads are made of concrete, but this road will be asphalt.
Asphalt is a mixture of cement and crushed stone or sand.

Workers lay down the asphalt with a paving truck. Then a roller rolls over the pavement, making it smooth and hard. After traffic lines are painted, the road is ready for cars!

In a city, a wall of wooden boards hides another construction site. No trees and boulders have to be removed from this site, but there is one thing still to be cleared—another building! This old parking garage will be torn down to make room for a new office building—a skyscraper.

PARK
HOUR·DAY
WEEK
RATES

How will they knock down a big building like this parking garage? First, a wrecking ball is attached to a ground crane. The crane swings the huge steel ball against the walls of the garage, smashing them to pieces. Trucks with hammer attachments break up floors and pavements. Some construction workers also use jackhammers to break apart the smaller pieces.

Backhoes dig a foundation for the new skyscraper. Then a pile driver is brought in. A pile driver hammers long steel posts into the ground, deeper and deeper, until the posts, called piles, hit hard rock. Piles spread the weight of the heavy building so that the ground and rock support it. Sometimes piles go as far down as 200 feet!

The frame of the skyscraper is already ten stories high. How do the workmen get building materials, like steel girders, up that high? They use a crane.

With its huge, strong hook, a crane lifts heavy girders and beams and sets them in place. When two cranes are needed, sometimes one crane will lift the other crane to a higher floor. Construction workers call this "jumping" the cranes.

A concrete mixer can't reach above the first floor of a skyscraper. That's why there is a special machine that carries concrete to the higher floors. It is called a concrete pump.

The concrete is taken to the construction site in a concrete mixer. Then the mixer pours the concrete into the back of the concrete pump. The pump forces the concrete up its long pipe. When the last bit of concrete is poured, the workers have a "topping out" ceremony. That means the skyscraper is finished!

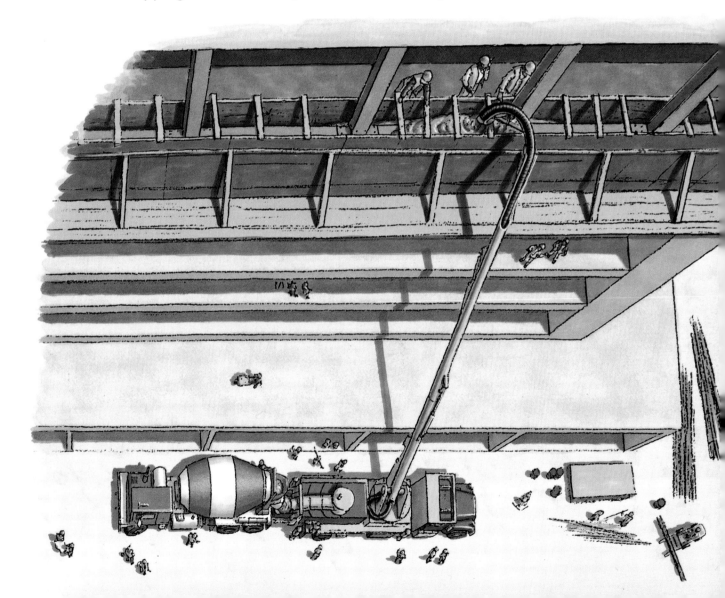

Hundreds of years ago, people had to build houses and buildings using just handheld tools. We're so lucky to have construction trucks today to help with the big jobs!